For Liam and Ellie, with love

(and to Sondre Norheim, the father of skiing.)

Published by Cerulean Blue
www.cblueepub.com

Text and Illustrations copyright © 2012 Annie B. Fox

All rights reserved. No part of this book my be used or reproduced in any manner whatsoever without written permission except in the case of brief quotations within critical articles and reviews.

Find out more about Sonder by visiting: **www.sonderthesnowsnake.com**

Find out more about *Save The Snow Snakes • Climate Education Fund* by visiting: **www.savethesnowsnakes.org**

Printed in Hong Kong

Summary: Sonder is a cute, furry snake who lives in the snowy mountains. He has no patience to learn the things he wants to do well, like playing in the snow and skiing with children. After crashing he embraces Zen-like lessons from his grandma, and becomes very good at many things.

ISBN 978-1-60530-094-8
[1. Skiing--fiction. 2. Snow--fiction 3. Patience--fiction]
I. Fox, Annie B. II. Title

Annie B. Fox

Sonder is a special little snake. Unlike other snakes, Sonder doesn't live in the hot dry desert or the wet rain forest. Instead, Sonder lives in the snow and ice. Other snakes like sunning themselves on warm rocks. Sonder loves licking icicles and having a frozen nose. What makes Sonder really different is his thick, white fur. Sonder is a snow snake.

In a cozy den beneath the snow, Sonder lived with his "Grandslither"—this is what snakes call their grandmas. Sonder knew Grandslither was good at just about everything a snow snake should be good at. And he knew what she loved best: to sit quietly and watch the falling snow…or gaze at the moon in the forest…and breathe…and relax…and think about nothing at all.

Sonder loved to play in the snowy mountains. He tried to catch snowflakes on his long, red tongue

...but usually missed.

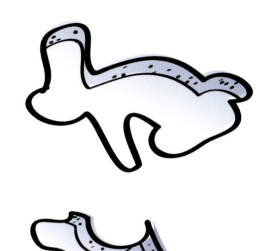

He tried to make snake-angels

in crusty old snow

…but they never looked right.

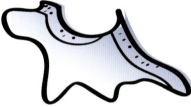
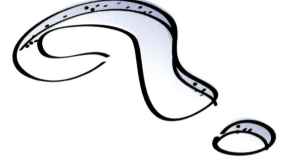

He tried to make tunnels under freshly fallen snow

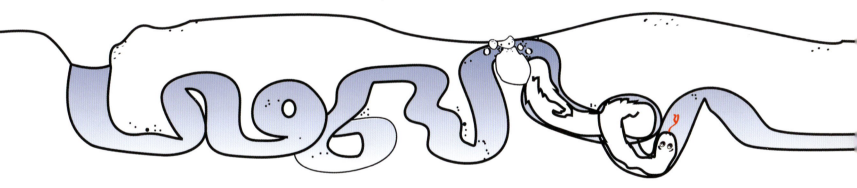

…but they always caved in and he got lost.

Grandslither said he needed to be more patient when he tried these things. *Patience? Humph*, he thought. Sonder just gave up. But secretly, he wished he could be really good at something.

One day, while the snow fell like feathers, Sonder went out exploring. He came to a wide clearing in the forest and stopped. He looked to the right and to the left, and tested the air with his tongue. Cautiously, he began to glide across the smooth snow, when he heard a *shuuuuushhhhhing* sound and laughter coming from the hill above. Suddenly a child came zooming by, followed by more children, all with boards strapped to their feet. Sonder was startled and ducked into the snow. When he was sure the children were gone, he peeked out. *That looked like fun,* he thought. *And they were very good at whatever it was they were doing.*

Sonder returned to the den, excited to tell Grandslither what he'd seen.

She explained that the children were skiing and snowboarding. "It's great fun for a snow snake to hold on to a child's boot and help them turn. If you would like, I can teach you how, but to do it well takes lots of practice."

Sonder couldn't wait for a lesson. *Practice? Humph,* he thought. He hid in the snow until a girl came along, twisting and turning on her skis. Just as she passed, Sonder swooped. CRASH! The girl, her skis, and Sonder went up in the air and they all landed. *Boom!*

The girl—who didn't see Sonder—brushed herself off and skied away. But Sonder was too shaken and bruised to try again, so he *slimped* (that's how a snake limps) back home.

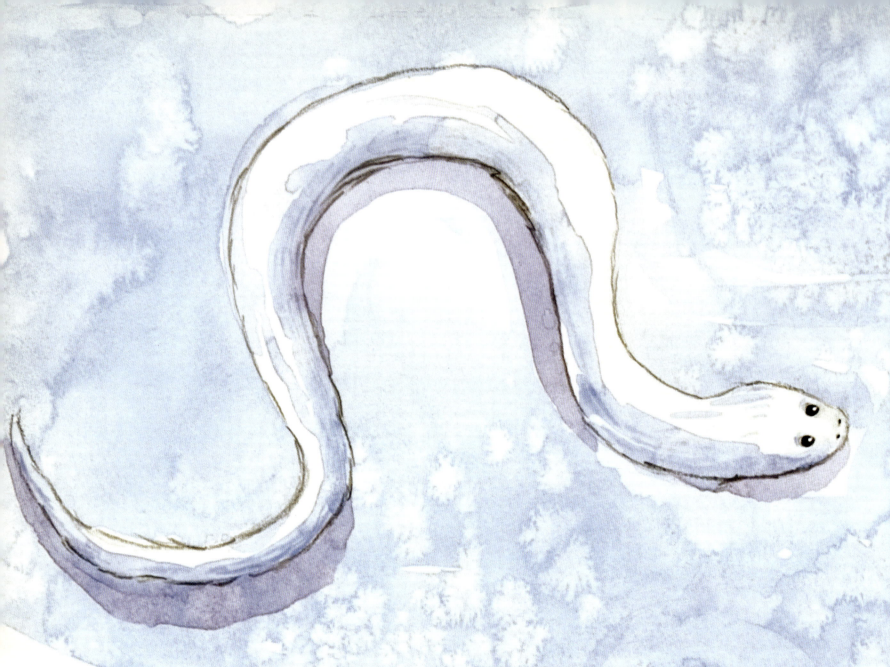

From the coziness of the cave Sonder recovered. He wanted to be good at something. Then he remembered the advice Grandslither had given him. "Would you please teach me how to ski with the children? I'll try to be patient and I will practice," he asked her. "Go clear your mind," she said. "Try to relax and listen. Think about the quiet beauty of the forest. When you have done this, come back."

Sonder practiced calming himself as Grandslither had told him to. He breathed slowly and deeply. Then he listened to the quiet sounds of winter. He spent a long time doing this and it did make him feel nice and calm.

Grandslither gave him another thing to practice: hiding in the snow. She whispered, "Master one thing, and then you are ready for the next."

As the months went by Sonder followed Grandslither's advice. Step by step he practiced all the things she taught him like lining up straight when a skier came along, jumping on, shifting his weight, and helping to keep the skiers and snowboarders from falling.

Sonder also practiced catching snowflakes on his tongue,

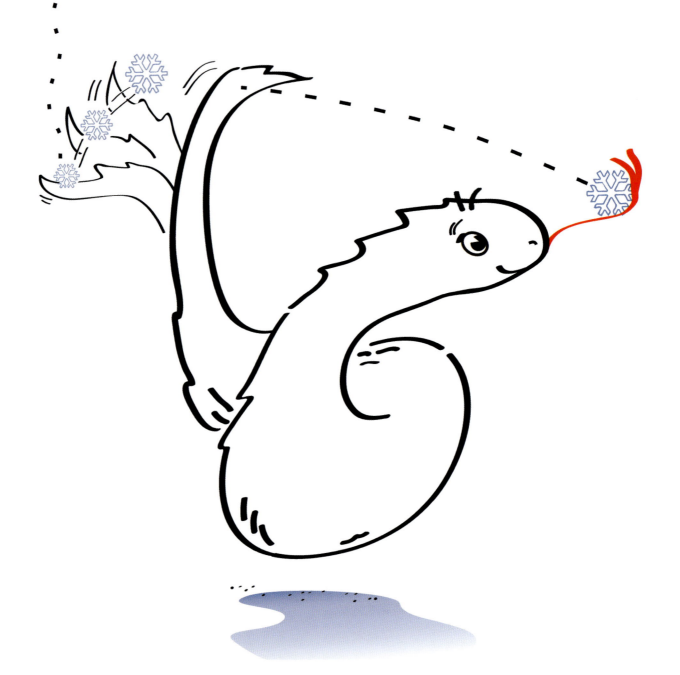

...making snake-angels that looked like they were supposed to,

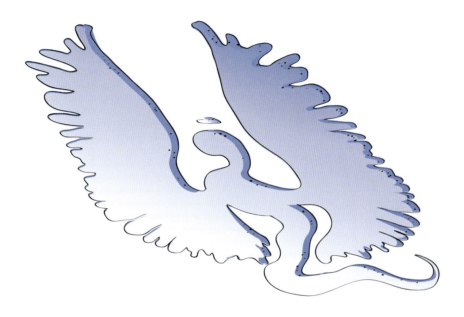

...and building miles of sturdy tunnels under the snow.

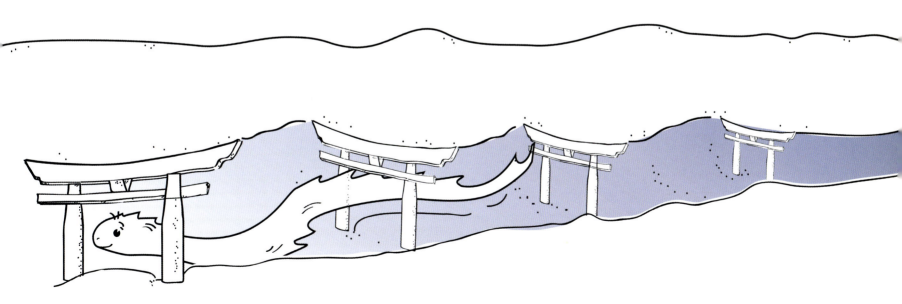

Each day Sonder practiced, and each day he got better. "Remember, nothing worth doing comes instantly. Everything lasting and worthy takes time and patience," he recalled Grandslither saying.

There came a day when Sonder was very good at what he did. He loved how the cold wind rushed through his fur when he went fast. He loved how his tummy felt when he made big swooping turns or went off a jump. When he was skiing or snowboarding there was nothing else that mattered to him besides the child and the snow.

To this day, Sonder may be playing somewhere in the snow, or expertly riding through the winter woods on someone's skis or snowboard. Or perhaps, he may be found calmly sitting and watching the falling snow …or gazing at the moon in the forest …and breathing …and relaxing …and thinking about nothing at all.

AFTERWORD

If snow snakes were real (and they are not) they would have especially hard heads. I did not draw Sonder wearing a helmet, but all children (and adults) should stay safe when skiing by always wearing a helmet and studying the rules of skiing safety. Find out more by visiting: www.lidsonkids.org

The snowy world that Sonder lives in *is* real and really is at risk. With the changing climate real creatures that are dependent on cooler temperatures are threatened. I have created a fund where 5% of the proceeds from the sale of this book will go to educate school children about the science of climate change and how they can make a difference. Find out more by visiting: www.savethesnowsnakes.org

This means "Snow" in Japaneese